This book belongs to

Written by Moira Butterfield
Illustrated by Simon Mendez

This edition published by Parragon in 2011
Parragon
Queen Street House
4 Queen Street
Bath BA1 1HE, UK

ISBN 978-1-4454-3463-6

Printed in China

Muddypaws

PaRragon

Bath • New York • Singapore • Hong Kong • Cologne • Delhi
Melbourne • Amsterdam • Johannesburg • Auckland • Shenzhen

It was a special day for Ben. He had a new puppy!
"I'll teach you all the things I know," said Ben.
"But first I need to choose a name for you. I'll need
to think hard about it. It has to be just perfect."

"I don't really mind what name you choose, as long as you give me lots of cuddles," thought the new puppy.

Ben looked around his bedroom to see if he could find an idea for the perfect puppy name.

"I'll look in my storybook," he said, but none of the names in the book were right for his new puppy.

"I think I'll leave you to hunt for names," thought the new puppy. "I'd rather look behind that flowerpot."

The little puppy crept over...

He sniffed...

...and then
he climbed.

He didn't mean to knock the flowerpot over, but...

Oops!

That's just what he did.

He made muddy pawprints everywhere.

"Let's go to the park. I might be able to think of a good name there," said Ben.

"I'd rather look behind that tree," thought the little puppy.

So he ran...

...and he ran.

He didn't mean to jump
in the mud, but...

squelch!

That's just what he did.

He made muddy pawprints everywhere.

Ben's neighbors were having a party in their backyard. "One of the guests might be able to think of a good name for you," said Ben. "Let's go and ask them."

"I'd rather look in the pond," thought
the new puppy.

So he leaned over...

...and he leaned over a little bit more.

He didn't mean to fall in the pond,
but...

Splosh!

That's just what he did.

He made muddy pawprints eVerywhere.

"We'd better go home and clean you up," said Ben.
    "I'd rather go digging in the backyard," thought the new puppy.

So he dug...

...and he dug...

...and he dug.

This time he found
lots of things...

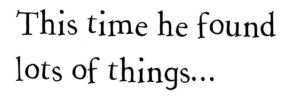

...a lost ring...

...an old wrench...

...and a toy car that Ben had lost.

He didn't mean to bring all
that mud indoors, but...

Pitter Patter!

... that's just what he did.

He made muddy pawprints everywhere.

And he didn't mean to find a name for himself at last, but... Guess what? That's *just* what he did!

"You are the muddiest, funniest puppy there ever was. There's only one name for you," laughed Ben.

"Muddypaws!"